Let's Go
TRICK-OR-TREATING!

By Lori Haskins Houran
Illustrated by Joanie Stone

A GOLDEN BOOK • NEW YORK

Text copyright © 2021 by Lori Haskins Houran
Cover art and interior illustrations copyright © 2021 by Joanie Stone
All rights reserved. Published in the United States by Golden Books, an imprint of
Random House Children's Books, a division of Penguin Random House LLC, 1745 Broadway,
New York, NY 10019. Golden Books, A Golden Book, A Little Golden Book, the G colophon,
and the distinctive gold spine are registered trademarks of Penguin Random House LLC.
rhcbooks.com
Educators and librarians, for a variety of teaching tools, visit us at RHTeachersLibrarians.com
Library of Congress Control Number: 2020934947
ISBN 978-0-593-17464-7 (trade) — ISBN 978-0-593-17465-4 (ebook)
Printed in the United States of America
10 9 8 7 6 5 4 3

"WHAT SHOULD WE BE THIS YEAR?"

my brother, Nick, asks me.

"How about monsters?" I say. "Or robots?"

We always wear matching Halloween costumes. Our parents used to pick them out. They dressed us up like pumpkins and puppies.

Now we get to choose. But sometimes it's hard to decide.

"Toby, look!" Nick calls. "We can be dinosaurs!"

Nick tries on a T. rex head. I go for the triceratops.

We each give a loud ROAR.

"You look great," Dad says. "Very scary!"

On Halloween night, we put on our costumes.
Then we grab our candy buckets.

"Let's go trick-or-treating!" I yell as I race Nick
out the door.

"Wait! Pictures first." Mom gets her camera.
Nick and I grin as she takes some photos.
"Excellent," Mom says. "Now you can go."

We run down the sidewalk and knock on the Chungs' door.

"Trick or treat!" we shout.
"My goodness, I thought dinosaurs were extinct," says Mrs. Chung. "But here are two big ones on my porch!"

She drops packs of
candy corn into our
buckets.
    "Boys, what do you
say?" Dad reminds us.
    "Thank you!" we
call out.

No one is home at the Johnsons' house.
But there's a big bowl of lollipops on the step.
I scoop up a handful. So does Nick.

"Just one!" says Mom.

Oops. I keep a chocolate lollipop and put the rest back. Nick picks cherry.

We go all the way down one side of our street, knocking on doors.

There are trick-or-treaters everywhere. Pirates and wizards. Superheroes and mummies. Vampires and . . . PINEAPPLES?

But no dinosaurs. I like that we're the only dinos in the neighborhood.

The last house on the street is a haunted house.
It's not really haunted. Mrs. Porter, our school
nurse, lives there. She just makes it look spooky.

A witch on the front porch waves to us.
"Come in! Come in!" she says.
The witch has glasses just like Mrs. Porter's.

Inside, it's kind of dark. Bats and spiderwebs hang from the ceiling. Two skeletons sit on the couch.
"BOO!" yells a ghost.
"BOO!" I yell back.

So far, I'm not afraid.

Then—something furry touches my leg!
"Eeeeek!" I scream.

It's just Mrs. Porter's dog, Muffin.
Everybody laughs.

"You scared me, buddy!" I scratch Muffin's ears. Nick rubs his belly. Then we wave goodbye to the ghost.

"Okay, guys," Dad says. "Let's try the other side of the street."
Officer Jan stops the cars so we can cross.

We trick-or-treat the whole way home.
We get more candy. LOTS and LOTS of candy.
"My bucket's full," Nick says.
Mine is, too. I can hardly lift it!

At home, we empty our buckets onto the table.
We split up the candy. Nick likes gummy worms,
jelly beans, and taffy. I love everything chocolate.

"You can each have three pieces tonight,"
Dad says, "if Mom and I can eat one, too!"
"What do you say?" I remind them.
"Please?" asks Mom.
"No, not that!" says Nick.

We both say . . .

"TRICK-OR-TREAT!"